I Can Read!™
Picture Book

The Berenstain Bears' SEASHORE TREASURE

Stan & Jan Berenstain

BARNES & NOBLE

NEW YORK

The Bear family was going to the seashore.

They were going across a bridge.

The bridge went to Laughing Gull Island.

It was called Laughing Gull Island

because so many laughing gulls lived there.

"*Ha! Ha! Ha!*" cried the laughing gulls

as they sailed across the sky.

"Will we be there soon?" asked Sister Bear.

"Yes," said Papa Bear.

"Do you see that house on the beach?

That is where we are going to stay."

The Bear family unpacked the car.

They carried their things into the house.

Brother, Sister, and Papa Bear

put on their swimsuits.

Mama decided to wait until later.

"Come, Papa," said Brother.

"Let's go to the beach."

"Hmm," said Papa.

"I found something in the closet."

"What is it?" asked Brother.

"It is a map," said Papa.

"An old pirate treasure map."

"Really, my dear," said Mama.

"It says this place used to be called

Pirates Cove!" said Papa.

"It says that pirates buried their booty here."

"What is booty, Papa?" asked Sister.

"It is treasure," said Papa.

"Pirate treasure. You know—gold, silver, diamonds, and rubies."

"Now, really, my dear," said Mama.

"Do you think the map is real?"

asked Brother.

"There's only one way to find out,"

said Papa. "Follow me."

Papa got a shovel.

They went down to the beach.

It was a bright sunny day.

The sea sparkled.

Waves crashed upon the shore.

"*Ha! Ha! Ha!*" cried the laughing gulls.

Papa began to dig.

The cubs splashed in the sea.

"Have you found any treasure yet, Papa?"

asked Brother.

"Not so far," said Papa.

"All I have found are some old shells."

"What is this one, Papa?"

asked Sister.

"That is a clam shell," said Papa.

"It is big and gray," said Sister.

"What is this one?"

asked Brother.

"That is an oyster shell,"

said Papa.

"It is bumpy and black,"

said Brother.

Papa looked at the treasure map.

"Hmm," he said.

"This must not be the right spot."

19

He moved to another spot

and dug some more.

"Any treasure yet, Papa?"

asked Brother.

"No, just more old shells," said Papa.

"What is this one?"

asked Brother.

"That is a scallop shell,"

said Papa.

"It is pretty and pink,"

said Sister.

"What are shells for?" asked Brother.

"Shells are the homes

of some sea animals," said Papa.

"The clam shell was the home of a clam.

The oyster shell was the home of an oyster.

The scallop shell was the home of a scallop."

The sun shone down.

The sea sparkled.

Waves crashed upon the shore.

"*Ha! Ha! Ha!*" cried the laughing gulls.

"Papa, what happened to the clam, the oyster, and the scallop?" asked Sister.

"I guess maybe the laughing gulls got them," said Papa.

Papa looked at the map again.

"Hmm," he said.

"This must not be the right spot."

He went to another spot

and dug some more.

"Any treasure yet, Papa?" asked Sister.

"I'm afraid not," said Papa.

"Just some more old shells."

"You know something?" said Papa.

"Digging for treasure is hot work!"

"*Ha! Ha! Ha!*" cried the laughing gulls.

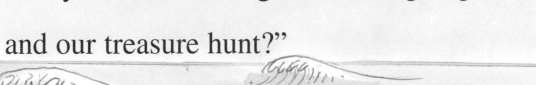

"Hmm," said Papa.

"Do you think those gulls are laughing at us

and our treasure hunt?"

"No way!" said Brother.

"We came looking for treasure

and we found it.

We found *the treasure of the sea*!"

"That's right," said Sister.

"A whole bucket full!"

"Time for a dip!"

said Papa.

After they cooled off

they headed back to the house

to show Mama their treasure.

"Papa," said Brother, "what are you going to do with the treasure map?"

"Hmm," said Papa, "I may just leave it in the closet for the next papa bear."